This book
belongs to:

First edition published in 2019 by Flying Eye Books,
an imprint of Nobrow Ltd. 27 Westgate Street, London E8 3RL.

1 3 5 7 9 10 8 6 4 2

Published in the US by Nobrow (US) Inc.
Printed in Latvia on FSC® certified paper.

ISBN: 978-1-911171-79-9
www.flyingeyebooks.com

SANG MIAO

THE IMMORTAL JELLYFISH

FLYING EYE BOOKS

LONDON | NEW YORK

A boy and his grandpa sat drawing together one afternoon.

"Have you ever heard of the jellyfish that lives for ever?" Grandpa asked.

"No, Grandpa. What is that?" replied the boy.

"It's called the immortal jellyfish. Whenever it seems like it is about to die, it starts its life again," smiled Grandpa.

“What about us? Are we immortal?” the boy enquired.

“Not in that way,” replied Grandpa.
“But there are other ways of living for ever.”

The boy did not understand. He wanted to be immortal,
and he wished his grandpa would tell him how.

But that week, he didn't see his grandpa at all. His parents said that his grandpa had died and that he would not be able to see him again.

SUNDAY

The boy felt lost.

That night, he cried quietly as
he drifted into a deep slumber.

Suddenly, he heard a familiar voice calling his name. It was his grandpa!

“Come on!” Grandpa said. “Put on your raincoat, we have to catch the last rainstorm!”

The boy hurried along behind him.

"Where are we going?" asked the boy.

"I'm going to show you how to become immortal!" Grandpa replied.

"Hold on tight!" shouted Grandpa
as a strong wind came from behind
and lifted them high into the sky.

As they flew higher and higher, the boy realised they were not in the sky at all, but in the ocean!

On the back of a great whale, they rode
through the big sea-sky. In the distance,
the boy could see a mysterious yellow door.

Beyond the door, they discovered a great
and beautiful world, bursting with life.

“Here we are!” said Grandpa.

In front of them, a smartly-dressed owl appeared.
"Hello!" it said, "Welcome to the Life Transfer City."

“This is a world of dreams, where the departed can live on through the memories of their loved ones.”

“Here you will find every kind of animal. They have all come here to be born again.”

“Each animal will choose a new creature to become, who will visit their family and friends in their dreams.”

"In this room, there is a creature inside every tube. Please follow me into the next room, where you can choose which one you would like to become."

As they entered, they met a man
who was choosing to become a fish.

He had been an accountant in his
previous life, memorising numbers
every day until he was quite exhausted.

He chose to become a fish, for it has a very short memory.

Then they met a lion, who had chosen to become a cloud.

The lion had been made to perform in the circus
and had no freedom whilst he was alive.

He chose to become a cloud so he could drift freely through the world.

Finally, the boy and his grandpa floated to the top of the great room. Here, all kinds of animals were being picked up and carried away to their new dreams by fantastic flying creatures.

Grandpa smiled and turned to the boy.
"It's time for me to make my decision, and for you to go home. I will see you again soon."

And with that, a beautiful white bird arrived to carry the boy home.

Together they flew over the
enchanting trees of the forest . . .

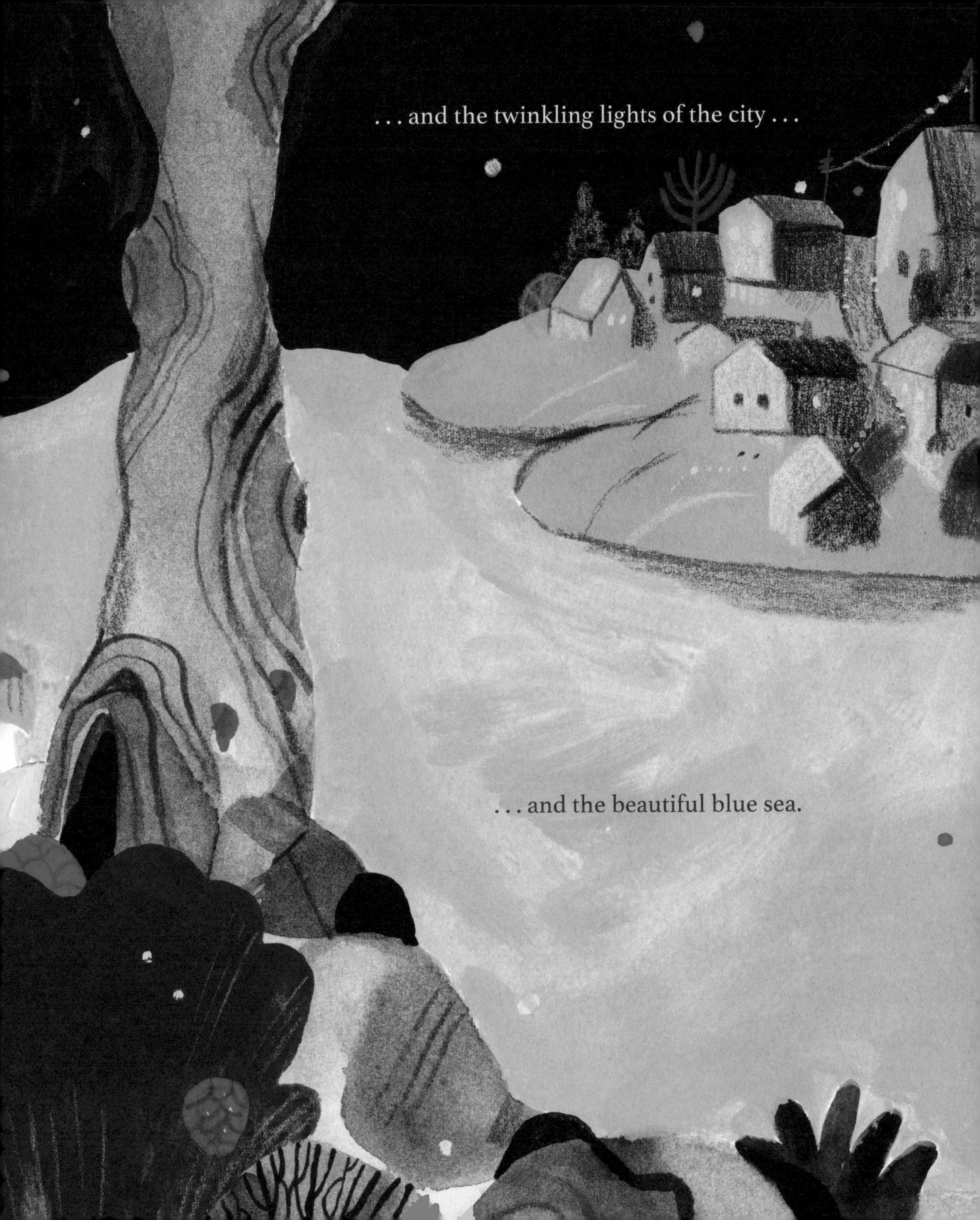

. . . and the twinkling lights of the city . . .

. . . and the beautiful blue sea.

Before he knew it, the boy was back in his own cosy bed,
wondering what his grandpa might choose to become.
Perhaps he would find out in his dreams.

A bird?

A fox?

A tree?

Or maybe . . .

. . . an immortal jellyfish.